THE MAGIC IN YOU

Written and Illustrated by

Emma Maree

FINGER FACTORY

onion PRINT

This story is dedicated to Mike Usher & all the children of Belize.
May they always think big and know that they are the leaders of A New World.

Contact Info
emma-maree@live.ie
www.emaree.com
Susan@susanmorrice.com
www.susanmorrice.com
ISBN #978-0-9571540-0-1

IF you look at the world, now don't get me wrong! Of course I don't mean for you to hop into the nearest rocket or spaceship and take a trip to outer space so you can see it from there! A simple picture will do. IF you don't have one on you right now you are welcome to use mine!

Turn to the next page if you please...

NORTH
AMERICA

BELIZE

SOUTH
AMERICA

AN

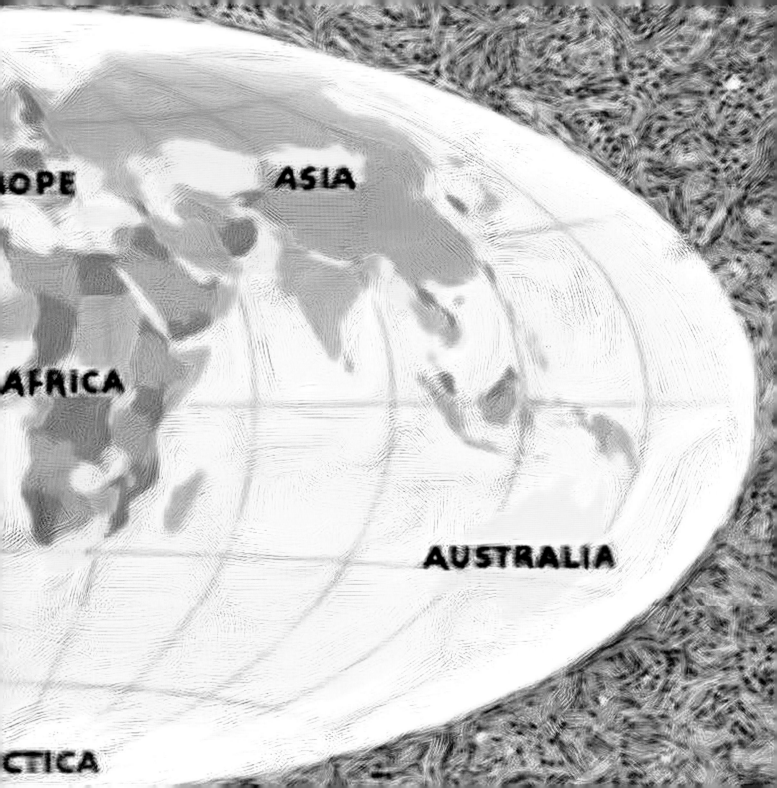

That was the world...
But you knew that right? Because I'm sure you have a pretty good idea what your own world looks like! Did you notice the black spot with an arrow pointing to it?

You did??!!

That is where the country of Belize is and it has always been there!

In the following story you read a tale of magic, some more magic and then a little bit more magic...
Magic can happen anywhere in the world and in this story it starts in Central America.

...Oh, and if you have any questions best wait until the end and then don't ask them, someone might see you talking to a book that doesn't answer back.

IT all started in Belize in the little village of Ladyville. It was a most beautiful place to grow up in with lots of wonderful colours to look at! But the best thing of all about Ladyville was...

...it was so close to the sea that you could taste the salt in the air and so close to the moon that you could say hello...

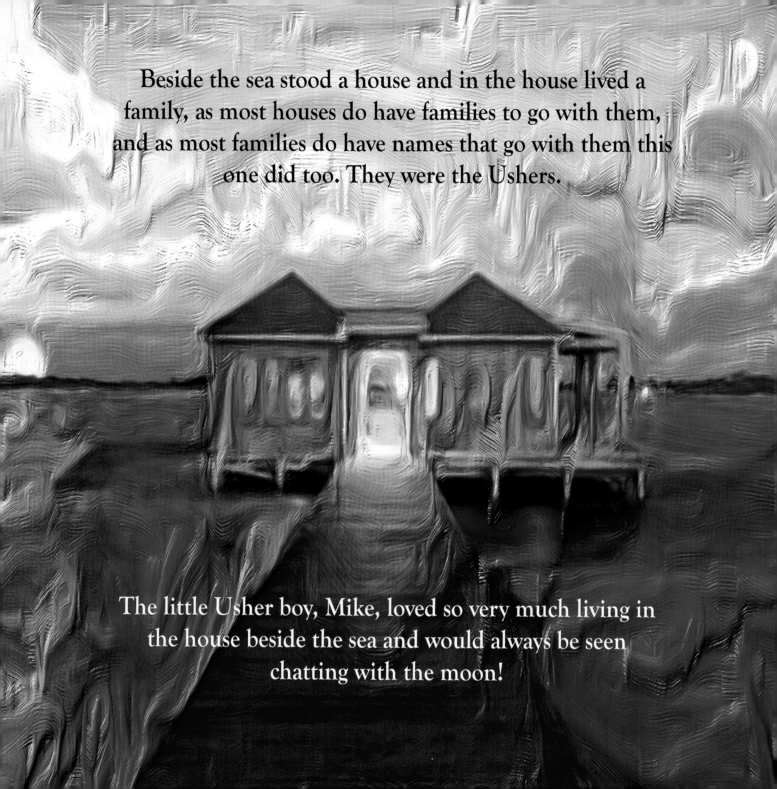

Beside the sea stood a house and in the house lived a family, as most houses do have families to go with them, and as most families do have names that go with them this one did too. They were the Ushers.

The little Usher boy, Mike, loved so very much living in the house beside the sea and would always be seen chatting with the moon!

"That boy has such big dreams in his head for such a small size!" Mike's father would say to his wife over supper.

"Why do you look at the moon so seriously?" His mother asked her little Usher one twilight.

"Momma, the moon and I do have the most spectacular conversations, and just now he told me the most important thing he has ever said!"

"Is it a secret?" His mother asked.

"Oh no, it most definitely must not be a secret ever! In fact the whole world needs to know about this one!"

"Come on then boy, spill the beans!" Mike's father said impatiently.

"There's magic liquid underneath Belize that gives energy to the world and he said that if I believe with all my heart, I will be able to bring it up to the people."

The belief in Mike's little face was the purest thing his parents had ever seen, he spoke to them with certainty in his voice and big wide puppy dog eyes.

"He also said that when the time is right some very magical people will walk into my life and will want to help me dig a hole in the ground so we can get to the river of liquid gold. Isn't that cool..." he said with a smile.

"Magic liquid?" Mr Usher looked at his wife, puzzled.

"He means oil dear" she said with a smile.

"Oh I see, well isn't that sweet" He said as he continued eating and nothing more on the matter was said...

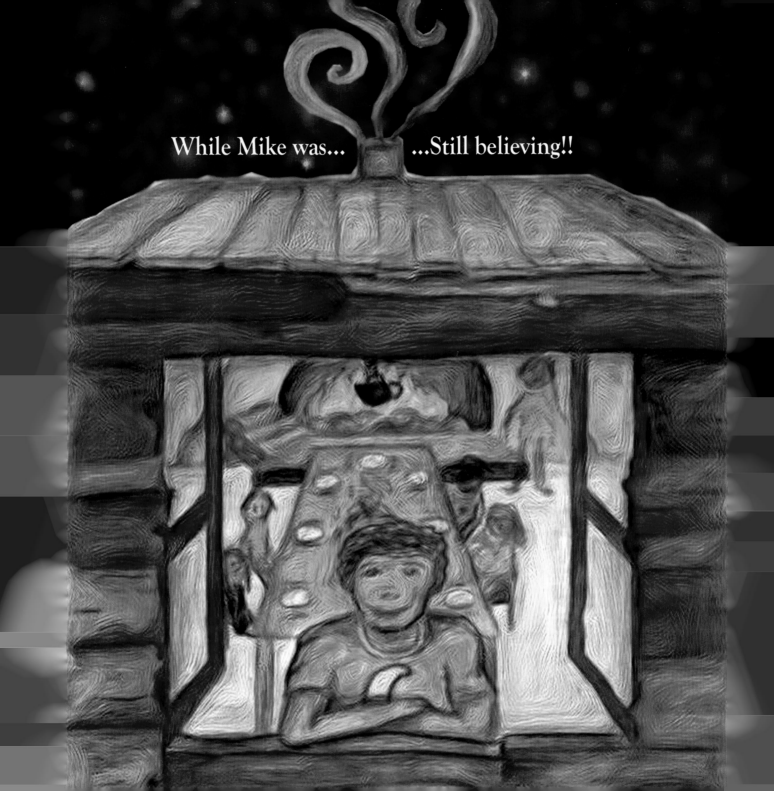

While Mike was...   ...Still believing!!

Years passed and the moon came and went thousands of times and the little Usher boy grew bigger and wider and taller and smarter! Then one day he and his lovely new wife left Ladyville and went to explore the world!

From their adventures Mike and his wife would send back letters to the house beside the sea and news would reach them of the greedy experts who had come to Belize with giant drills and put holes in the ground to see if they could find the magic liquid to take back for themselves!

"If we find oil here we will be filthy rich Mawhawhawhaa!!!"

But the greedy experts had to leave Belize after years of searching and never finding a drop!

"There is no oil here!!! It's no good, lets go home!"

The time had come for Mike and his wife to return to the place they loved the most, Belize.

"A long time ago when I was a little boy the moon told me there were rivers of liquid magic underneath Belize and despite the greedy experts that have tried and failed I
believe that I will find it and make a difference for the whole country!" Mike told his wife on their return.

"I believe!"

So Mike was now back in Belize. The ground was dry and the sun was keeping his back hot when he was busy
looking for the magic. Then, just like the moon had said, a very magical lady walked into his life.

"Hello! Are you the man who believes that there are magic rivers of liquid gold running underneath Belize?
My name is Susan and I have a special way of knowing if there is magic hidden in the ground just by looking at the rocks! Why don't we have a wee look...?!"

Mike was amazed that this happy lady who always jumped into everything with enthusiasm, was bursting to help him!

So Mike and Susan joined forces and looked at all the rocks in Belize. Mike was overjoyed that he had now found a kindred spirit in Susan who shared his dream for the country.

After looking at rocks for many years, Susan told Mike that she too was absolutely certain that the magic was underneath the ground and that she would help for as long as it took to bring it up!

But Mike had noticed something else in Susan too...

"The more I get to know you Susan the clearer it becomes that you possess some sort of magic inside of you! You're different to most people I know, what is it? " Mike asked his fellow friend!

"You know Mike, I'm glad you asked me that," she smiled.

"I can tell you the answer, you see its not just underneath rocks and in the heat of the sun that the energy and the magic of the world lies, but inside each and every living being on this earth shines a very powerful light that is unlimited."

Immediately Mike felt a little tickle in his stomach. He was sure as Susan spoke these words that it was truth! He straight away believed that this energy inside of him was just like the oil underneath Belize.

"The oil within," he said.

He knew that just like finding it in the ground would make a difference to a whole country, finding it in him would make a difference to the whole world!

"Well, I know of an enchantingly charming magical magician called Merlquin.

He teaches people how to access and use their own magic, he can teach you too if you'd like!?"

With ONE move Mike jumped from his seat and shouted...

"Yes!"

So Susan and Mike hopped into Susan's amazingly super transporting machine and flew to Paradise, the place where Merlquin lived.

When the enchantingly charming magician Merlquin laid eyes on Mike for the first time he was blinded by the white light that was shining out of him.

Immediately Merlquin knew that the ideas that Mike had in his head were so powerful that they could change the world so he listened very carefully to every word Mike had to say.

Mike told Merlquin about the many conversations he had with the moon when he was a small boy.

"Ah, yes, well the moon is a very clever fellow you know, if he told you there was oil in Belize then there most definitely is!"
Merlquin nodded.

For the next two weeks Merlquin taught Mike how to access the unlimited powers that lay unused inside him. "Wow, this is amazing. I never knew just how magic I am inside, and to think that ALL the people in the world have these powers too and they just don't know it!" Mike was excited about this and wanted the world to know what he knew. He decided that he would send his family to Merlquin with a view to them sending their friends and so on. Pass it on. He learned how to focus ALL of his mind on one thing by becoming more aware of ALL he sees, hears, feels, tastes and smells and many more magical tools to use in his life day to day. After two weeks Mike was ready to leave Merlquin and the Island, which truly was paradise, and return home. He had unlocked his magic inside and was convinced that he would now easily bring up the magic that lay under Belize.

As they said their goodbyes, Merlquin told Mike one last magic spell...
"Now just remember to think backwards, see your dream clearly in your mind as though it has happened then just take the next step you see in front of you and the road will be lighted for you."
This was the most important spell that Mike had learned.

Straight away Mike closed his eyes and imagined that the magic liquid was gushing out of the earth, he could hear the people cheering, feel his own and their excitement. He could smell the oil and taste the champagne on his tongue that is for the celebrations!
"Aha, the sweet taste of success" he said to himself smiling.

Without delay Mike knew what the next step was.

"We need to find a bunch of people who will help us build a giant drill so we can drill a huge hole in the ground."

"Okay!" Susan had an idea.

'Mike did I ever tell you about the mystical land across the Atlantic Ocean called Ireland? That's where I lived when I was a little girl! Merlquin used to live there too! I know hundreds of enchanting folk who just like me and you have learned how to use their own magic. I know in my heart that they would love to be a part of this amazing adventure!"

"Susan that sounds like a wonderful idea! Let's go to Ireland!" Mike jumped up ready to go.

...And so, Mike accompanied Susan back to her homeland where a very large party was taking place...

Susan quickly joined in while Mike was still getting out of the amazingly super transporting machine.

"What's going on here? What is the party for?" Mike asked the first person who stopped for a moment.

"We're celebrating!" A little jolly fellow sang in the key of C.

"Well I can see that, but for what?"

"Life!" The little guy answered.

"Just life! Wahoo" he grabbed Mikes hands and swung him into a circle of people dancing and singing. He couldn't help but hop and skip around with the music.

The blissful merriness was quite contagious and for a brief moment Mike had forgotten why he came there in the first place until he heard Susan shout from the top of a very large mushroom, "I think we've found what were looking for Mike, do you agree?" as she continued to dance.

"Oh yes indeed Susan, yes indeed"
he agreed wholeheartedly.

They had stumbled upon the very magical folk they were looking for and straight away they had their team with one clear invincible vision, to bring the magic up to the people of Belize.

So they all headed off together on one big adventure to build one big giant drill!

Everyone got to work straight away!

They all had their own special jobs and each person was so overflowing with passion for their job that nothing could possibly go wrong but then sadly all of a sudden Mike became sick. Then he became a lot sicker and

decided it was best that he left this world but all the while still believing even more than ever that the day when the magic would be brought up was coming closer; even closer than Susan and the mystical Irish folk knew.

Everyone missed Mike very much but knew that
working harder and making his dream come true
would make him eternal and everyone in Belize
would know the name of the little Usher boy who
had such big dreams in his head for
such a small size!

For one whole year after Mike died everyone worked and worked. They looked at rocks and built the giant drill and now the time had come to put the hole in the ground. The only problem was that they could not all agree where to put the hole.

The night before the hole was to be made the mystic Irish folk and the people of Belize were to have a huge party to celebrate the dig! Susan was on her way to the party with her little girl Clare.

In a moment of bother Susan stopped her car on a little bumpy road and got out! She looked up to the night sky who was gathering her stars.

"Oh night sky, if only we knew exactly where to put the hole, for those silly experts sneered and said it would take fifteen holes to find the oil if there is any at all!" Susan said to the sky but was distracted by a little tug on her hand, she looked down...

"Momma, the moon told me that there is magic right here where we are standing, underneath the ground." Clare told her mother sweetly.

"Wow! Thank you Clare"
Susan hugged her and then looked up to the sky.
"Thank you moon... Thank you Mike!"
She said with a wink and a smile.

The next day at nine o'clock after much excitement and a lot of magic from a lot of people with ONE clear vision... A hole was made in the ground of Belize beside a very bumpy road and the purest, very best oil gushed out of it like magic!

The most magical thing of all was that it was exactly one year to the day that Mike had died...

...And now, through his biggest achievement, he would live forever.

THE BEGINNING

The true story behind Belize oil

In 1988 Mike Usher met Irish-American Susan Morrice who is a geologist. He had met a kindred spirit in Susan who believed in his dream. She went to Belize and over the next fifteen years they searched.

THE IMPOSSIBLE DREAM.

The background to this true story is that 50 oil companies over a period of years had all searched for oil in Belize and failed. More and more Mike's great dream for oil and a new Belize seemed impossible. Then they met Dr Tony Quinn. Dr Tony Quinn specialises in teaching 'how to use more of your mind. Then how to apply the 'more' to everyday life and goals.' Obviously our mind plays a crucial role in every moment of our lives. Therefore if we increase its power we soon see the Difference. The essence of Tony's approach is where he helps people to super concentrate their mind-power and focus it on their major goals. He maintains that then the desired goals will be installed in their mind and the desired results will follow. Mike made the decision to take one of Dr Tony Quinn's seminars.

MORE DREAMERS

After Mike had attended the seminar they were convinced that they had now found the secret to success and founded Belize Natural Energy. The only problem was that they needed money. It would take millions of dollars to drill but at this point the big oil companies just laughed at them. Left with nowhere else to turn to they began to tell their story to people who also attended the seminars and understood this 'secret to success'.
Over time 76 people became investors. A unique group of people in particular Sheila McCaffery (Irish) - Jean Cornec (French), Paul Marriott (English) - Alex Cranberg (American) took the dream to their hearts and applied all of their minds to it along with Mike and Susan. Dr Tony Quinn was also now on board and everything was in place and B.N.E were ready to strike oil!
While this was going on Mike began to feel unwell. Over a three month period he went down hill and then died. Everyone involved was shocked by Mike's death but by this time his great dream had taken on a life of its own.

A NEEDLE IN A HAYSTACK!!

B.N.E purchased a lease on approximately 500,000 acres of land over 8 years. This left only enough money to drill two wells. Imagine the picture, 500,000 acres and somewhere in this vast area you're going to drill a 20 inch wide hole in the hope of finding oil. B.N.E started drilling in June 2005 and on the 24th at 9 o'clock in the evening they struck oil and it was exactly on the first anniversary of Mike's death.

THE USHER GUSHER

Through the application of Dr Tony Quinn's Educo seminar Mike and Susan had realised the impossible, an oil strike in one. What else could they call the first well but Mike Usher #1...

L-R : Mike Usher, Dr Tony Quinn, Susan Morrice

Then the impossible happened four more times in a row! In the oil business on average you have to drill 15 wells before you strike oil. B.N.E oil is what is known in the trade as Light Crude, the most desirable of all oils. The growth of B.N.E has been phenomenal. The company was exporting oil within four months of the discoveries, which is unheard of in the international oil field (it can sometimes take years) and with no infrastructure in the country.

THE OIL BUSINESS

The staff quickly grew to over 200 of which 95% are Belizean. A Chief Executive Officer was needed to head up the company, someone who knew the country, its people and above all, someone who believed in Mike's dream of a new and better Belize and could carry it into the future. In September 2006, Dr Gilbert Canton became C.E.O. He has proven to be an invaluable leader and is totally committed to the mission of the company.

THE OIL WITHIN

The philosophy of the company is that we all have oil within us in the form of our dreams. Just like the oil in the ground, while it was always there it takes the right mind-set to draw it out.
It all started with a man who believed in something and he inspired a group of people, ultimately they became one mind. However it was not until they learned how to super-concentrate their belief did it have enough power to draw out the oil. The degree of power is the dividing line between success and failure. When our belief in our dreams becomes mixed with doubts, fears and negative mind-sets then they become weak wishes with no power. The oil discovery is a beacon to Belize and the world as an example of the power of belief. If you too want to strike oil you must invest all of your mental energy in your dream so powerful that all doubts fall away from it. Only pure belief can breath life into your dreams and they become reality.
Like Mike, your dream may become immortal and unlimited. Immortal because Mike gave life to his dream and now it lives on beyond his lifetime and this oil discovery will go down in history as a turning point in Belize.
Unlimited because Mike's dream was never just about oil but also about the human spirit and potential within us, which is unlimited.
Whenever this story is told whether it be in a Newspaper, on a billboard or in a children's book it will inspire people to believe in themselves, their dreams and what is possible. The story goes out like a mighty wave of 'Belize Natural Energy' and pushes back the weeds of doubt and causes people and dreams to flower everywhere!
"All things are possible to him that believeth"
-Jesus (Mark 9:23)